IDENTITY CHRONICLES

A LIFE CHANGING SAGA PART1

ABHINAV KRISHNA
RAYACHOTI

Made with ♥ on the Notion Press Platform
www.notionpress.com

This book is dedicated to each and every person who believes in the power of thoughts that can transform their lives and shape their future. My heartfelt gratitude towards my family for their unwavering support, without which this wouldn't have been possible.

Contents

FOREWORD

Every book carries a story beyond its pages—a journey of thoughts, experiences, and lessons woven together with purpose. Identity Chronicles is one such journey, born from a deep belief in the power of thoughts to transform lives and shape destinies.

As I set out to write this book, I was driven by a desire to explore the profound impact of self-discovery, resilience, and the unseen forces that guide us. The words within these pages are not just reflections but invitations—to think, to dream, and to achieve something extraordinary.

Writing this book has been a transformative experience, one that required not just introspection but also unwavering support. My heartfelt gratitude goes to my family, whose belief in me has been a pillar of strength throughout this journey. Their encouragement has made every challenge feel surmountable, and every doubt turn into determination.

To every reader who picks up this book, I hope you find something that resonates, something that sparks a new way of thinking or affirms the path you are on. This book is not just mine—it belongs to everyone who believes in the endless possibilities of the mind.

With gratitude and hope,
Abhinav Rayachoti

PREFACE

Every individual embarks on a journey of self-discovery—an exploration of thoughts, emotions, and the choices that shape their identity. Identity Chronicles was born out of a deep curiosity about the power of thoughts and their ability to influence our reality. This book is not just a collection of words; it is a reflection of the struggles, revelations, and transformations that define who we are.

The idea for this book stemmed from my fascination with how our thoughts shape our perspectives and, ultimately, our lives. Throughout my writing journey, I encountered moments of doubt, uncertainty, and inspiration. But every challenge only strengthened my belief that thoughts are powerful enough to change the course of our destiny.

Through these pages, I invite you to dive into the depths of introspection, to question, to dream, and to embrace the endless possibilities that lie within you. This book is not about providing answers but about inspiring thoughts that lead to self-realization.

I extend my heartfelt gratitude to everyone who has been a part of this journey—my family, whose unwavering support has been my greatest strength, and every reader who chooses to embark on this journey with me. May these words resonate with you and inspire you to explore the boundless potential within.

Happy reading!

Abhinav Rayachoti

Acknowledgements

Writing Identity Chronicles has been an incredible journey, and I would not have been able to complete it without the support, encouragement, and guidance of many wonderful people.

First and foremost, my deepest gratitude goes to my family, whose unwavering belief in me has been my greatest source of strength. Your constant encouragement and support have made this journey possible.

A heartfelt appreciation to every reader who picks up this book. Your time, thoughts, and reflections mean the world to me. It is for you that I write, and I hope these pages resonate with you in a meaningful way.

I would also like to extend my sincere gratitude to Notion Press for providing a platform that empowers writers to bring their stories to life. Their tools and resources have made the publishing process seamless and accessible.

Lastly, to the unseen forces of creativity, perseverance, and inspiration that kept me going—this book is a testament to the power of thoughts, dreams, and the will to bring them to life.

With gratitude,
Abhinav Rayachoti

Prologue

We, in general, do not have an escape from the regular life and daily hustle. But what if we could transform our life to our tastes? What if life was perfect in every sense? What if we cherished every moment of it?

These are the questions that Aarav, a 19-year-old teenager, is yearning to know the answers to. Join the incredible journey of Aarav, where he longs for an escape from reality. But in his pursuit of something greater, he soon finds himself at the crossroads of choice and consequence.

As the world around him begins to shift in ways he never expected, one question lingers in his mind—is true happiness ever without a cost?

Delve into the fascinating world of Identity Chronicles - Part 1, the first installment of the Identity Chronicles series, which subtly encourages readers to view life from a broader perspective—beyond the daily hustle, struggle, and suffering.

I

“When are you going to rise above the ranks?” These were the words of Aarav Sen’s father, and he really meant it. The disappointment in his voice was palpable.

“I just cannot believe you said that!” Aarav retorted, his voice laced with mild frustration, and a feeble voice as he laid on the hospital bed, with the oxygen mask on his face.

Aarav’s father, who had just returned from a long, tiring day at work, and had to bring his son to the hospital soon after reaching home, heard his son’s complaint and started contemplating aloud. “Is he really our son? Such a timid, incompetent lad was unheard of in our families for quite a long time until now. The audacity to blame the world for his incapability in doing things!” he fumed, his temper flaring.

Aarav’s father was highly ill-tempered, and the rough phase he was going through at work certainly did not help things for Aarav.

Aarav took a deep breath and started contemplating on the things that took place in his life thus far...

He was quite sure that this was not what destiny had in store for him.

II

"A BABY BOY WOULD BRING JOY, PEACE AND HONOUR TO THE FAMILY. HE WOULD CARRY THE LEGACY FORWARD AND WOULD ONLY INCREASE THE STATURE OF THE FAMILY."

Monsoons were in full-swing in Mumbai, but the heat was on in the Sen's family, with each person in the family desperate for a baby boy, as an astrologer had predicted good times for them if a baby boy arrived at their house.

The Sen's family was a traditional family, strongly rooted in culture and ethics. They had ancestors who were great achievers, especially in the field of education. Education had never been neglected in the family, neither had discipline. Therefore, it was quite natural that these two qualities were strongly emphasised on as generations passed by.

Kuldeep Sen, in himself, was a highly acclaimed scholar, having graduated from one of the topmost institutes in the country and he was one of the rare persons in the family to pursue masters abroad in the United States of America. He had married at the age of 35 as he was adamant on achieving whatever his father wanted him to achieve first and only then, shall he marry.

Kuldeep's father was the founder of many educational institutions and was renowned for being a highly regarded professor himself. He had got himself a P.H.D in the field of mathematics, and was one of the finest mathematicians of his era. It only made sense that he expected his son, Kuldeep to outshine him and grow bigger, and the challenge was not only accepted by Kuldeep with aplomb, it was totally fulfilled too. Whether Kuldeep wanted something else in life or did he wish to do something else apart from his father's commands, well only Kuldeep knew the answer to that.

Surprisingly (or maybe not), he had found a perfect match in Nitya Shinde, who was another ambitious person who wouldn't put a step wrong to displease her father and had set her goals to have a respectable position in the society and then marry. Thus, it was pretty obvious that both the families were in talking terms on the marriage and it was all done before anyone realised.

Both the Shinde's and the Sen's were so similar, yet different. For instance, if one imagines the Sen's as striving for excellence, then the Shinde's family would be striving to also come out on top, no matter how you do it.

This analogy quite sums up the nature of the two families. One thing was clear-both strived for excellence. But it was the approach that was different.

This meant that there were obviously some disparities between them after the wedding. The Sens believed in hard work, no matter what the circumstances were. They were convinced that victory would be theirs as long as they remained honest and dedicated in their efforts. In contrast, the Shinde's took the opposite approach; they relied on shortcuts and cunning strategies to come out on top. What united these two families, nevertheless, was their unwavering faith on astrology and the never-ending respect towards their culture and tradition.

The so-called Kuldeep Sen and his father-in-law, in particular, were very nervous for probably the first time in their lives. The news would be out any minute and all the other members in the family, had their fingers-crossed.

Kuldeep heart skipped a beat as he saw the doctor come out of the operation theatre to make the announcement. The moment the entire family was waiting for had finally arrived; as for them it was a question of their future prospects, legacy and well-being. The big revelation was finally about to be made.

"HEARTY CONGRATULATIONS, MR. AND MRS. RANA, ON YOUR ADOPTION. MAY YOU HAVE A JOYOUS PARENTING JOURNEY AHEAD. BEST WISHES, AND I AM SURE YOU WILL INDEED TAKE GOOD CARE OF THIS LITTLE BOY RIGHT HERE. ALL SIGNS INDICATE HE IS FORTUNATE TO HAVE BEEN ADOPTED BY SUCH LOVELY PEOPLE."

The room buzzed with excitement as Mr. and Mrs. Rana held the little boy for the first time. Their eyes sparkled with tears of joy, and the air was filled with the warmth of heartfelt wishes and shared happiness.

The Ranas were well-known for their simplicity and kind-hearted nature. More importantly, both Harshit Rana and his wife, Deepika, understood the profound value of parenting, having both grown up without that vital aspect in their own lives.

Harshit Rana was often seen as a man written into a script of gut-wrenching tragedies, authored by fate itself. Left for adoption when he was only a 6-year-old by parents who felt he was a liability as he was underdeveloped and would only bring bad to the family's reputation and honour. Harshit spent his early years in childcare, longing for a sense of belonging. It wasn't until a teacher from the integrated school at the childcare centre noticed his exceptional talent in mathematics that Harshit's life began to change.

Harshit was adopted by this teacher at the age of eight, but not out of compassion or empathy; rather, she saw potential in him that could be monetized. Although this might sound bizarre, it was a harsh reality, or what Harshit has always assumed to be reality, now appears riddled with tiny fractures—moments where memory contradicts itself. Harshit was a prodigy in mathematics, effortlessly solving problems across a spectrum of complexities—from elementary multiplication to engineering-level vector calculus.

The relationship between Harshit and his adoptive mother resembled that of a celebrity and their manager, with one crucial difference: Harshit was never treated like a celebrity. His so-called mother was indifferent to his well-being, focusing solely on how to extract financial gain from his talents. She paraded him through talent shows and mathematics institutes, where Harshit gained recognition and she reaped the rewards.

Remarkably, Harshit never complained. He cherished the opportunities, grateful for the chance to showcase his talent on a grand stage. His happiness ignited from his passion, and he never questioned her decisions as they aligned with his interests. It feels remotely impossible to even think of such a pious man at this point of time in a world full of dishonesty, dissatisfaction and greed.

As years rolled by, Harshit's family of two became a respected household in society. By the age of 22, Harshit had founded his own mathematics institute, which rapidly gained prominence within a year of its establishment. He was hailed as the youngest entrepreneur, celebrated for his incredible achievement. Harshit was a beacon of inspiration, exemplifying how one's perspective on circumstances could lead to tremendous results.

However, life took another turn. Just a year after receiving the award, Harshit faced another blow when his mother passed away. He was heartbroken. Despite her viewing him as a mere financial asset, Harshit had no other figure to rely on. Yet, lack of a strong emotional bond allowed Harshit to eventually move on and start a new chapter in life.

He married Deepika, a journalist who had defied familial stereotypes that confined women to domestic roles. Deepika's family never desired a daughter, and consequently, a bond never developed between them. This made it easier for her to break free and pursue her passion, despite the challenges she faced. Her relentless pursuit of journalism, a career she loved, gave her a sense of fulfilment despite familial disapproval and the ever-coming obstacles

Harshit and Deepika shared common ground—both became highly successful through diligence and dedication to their passions, and both experienced a childhood devoid of parental affection. They resolved to adopt a child, ensuring he would never feel the absence of unconditional love and support. Their sole desire was for him to be happy and fulfilled.

That child is now, a 19-year-old author, who, defying all stereotypes, followed his heart and became successful in the path he chose, with no regrets whatsoever. All of this was possible, thanks to his wonderful parents, who never forced him into treading a known path or a safe option, rather, stood as pillars when he was trying to climb an unencountered peak.

In adopting me, Harshit and Deepika fulfilled their promise. At the age of one, I entered a world of heaven, embraced by parents who were angels in every sense.

My name is Anand, and as the name suggests, happiness rejuvenates in every ounce of my body.

IV

"Yet another nail in the coffin today. Another day passes by with me questioning my existence. Neither can I live a life my own, nor can I live my parents dream of. Is this how life is for others? I am sure I am not the only one trotting this untreaded path, and that is what scares me. Imagine dying one fine day and not having a single day worth reminiscing of the last few moments of your stay.... that is what painful death should be.... definitely fiercer and throbbing than a gunshot or a stab.

All I wish for is that one moment, where life comes to life. I know this seems like nitpicking, but these are the words of that one wounded soul which is on the brink of existence. It's not sure whether it can endure more suffering.

The suffering is mental, and I know these words are quite not what a 19-year-old should be drafting. However, this is not how world should be. The world is full of unreasonable expectations, suffocating responsibilities and toxic relationships- and it's only going downhill from here. How I hope there is something beyond life, something beyond this gut-wrenching sorrow, something that is idealistic not materialistic, something which a non-

programmed human being can cope with. Is there such a world that feeds people nectar, is there? Is there a world of embracement, encouragement and unconditional acceptance? Is there a place for a sparrow like me, wanting to be set free?

There shouldn't be. There definitely isn't. If there is, there is one only afterlife- beyond all science.

The days keep passing by, and I hope my time is near.............................. I cannot do this anymore; I think I have exhausted all the resilience ever left in me.

If only there was someone, I could lament my distress to, of course I am venting it out to you but you would really want to have a family member whom you could confide to. The irony here is that I am in such a dire state due to my family, which is funny, if you think about it.

Well, I am just kind of relieved that I have you, and you will have to bear with me for a while at least, although I do think my time is near, if this is how things are going to be.

The saddening part is that I don't find any solace in my college too- having friends is just an alien thing. More about this later.

What else would you expect if you are admitted in a top college even though you are not intellectually capable. I never wanted to get admitted here, but my father had other plans, although I could see the utter disgust in his face while he was seeking admission for me here via the 'not-so-worth-speaking-of' mode.

My family had decided I was a disgrace to their reputation, and what was worse is that all were in a consolidated agreement with it. I was bad at academics, you could say downright terrible, I was not good in any sport, I was an introvert, or rather should I say that I am still the same incapable idiot.

I do have my own aspirations, I mean who doesn't? But something worth noting here is that the affection my family has shown towards in every single walk of my life till now has made sure that I forget what my aspirations are.

Yes, it's true, although unfortunate. I don't remember what my aspirations are. It may sound obnoxious but these things do happen. I don't find a purpose of my living; probably except being a colossal disappointment. The fact I am just a burden to this family of pundits and intellectuals stings me harder, day by day, and the mental suffering was beyond comprehension.

Another thing I realised is that life is a template, at least from my experience. We are all puppets dancing to the tune of the master who sways our movements at random times in abysmal directions, and we have to keep quiet and bear the price, even though it can mean being broken down emotionally and mentally.

Is there another ideal, welcoming world? Is there? I would do anything to go there. God not forbid, I really wish I could just sleep and wake up there."

V

"What are you doing? Aren't your supplementary examinations approaching? The least you could do is stop being an abject failure and start putting sincere efforts to come back on track in life. If not carry forward our family's legacy, which you aren't worthy or capable of anyway, I think the least you could do is do yourself a favour, study hard, earn a professional degree, get a respectable job, so that people continue to spare some reputation for us in the not-so distant future. If not, I cannot see our family's reputation and honour go in shambles, so I may just disown you and leave you stranded on the streets."

Holding back tears was something Aarav was accustomed to, and he generally was mentally prepared to face the worst of the worst insults and criticism. However, his father words always took an ugly turn and had found to bring about tears of agony in his eyes.

Not that he wasn't trying to study anyways. It was just that he found academics to be extremely tedious and over-burdening. To draw parallels, academics to Aarav was what mental peace to his father- both of these things were elusive for them to gain, respectively.

Another note to consider here is that he just couldn't make up his mind to study no matter how much it mattered in his life. In fact, it was one of the only few things apart from discipline that was a mandate in the Sen's undeniable legacy.

"Your son Aarav is such a gem of a person, Mr. Kuldeep. I haven't seen any student of this age with such a calm demeanour and that sense of respect towards elderly people, quite remarkable, I must say."

"What use is of a candle if it looks decorated but does not produce light, Mr. Pathak? He is absolutely negligent and lazy towards his academics. May god put some sense into the lad's mind and make him pass the forthcoming semester examinations which is a very rare occurrence, hence it would only make sense to leave him under God's guidance. Which is why I have called you Mr. Pathak, I was wondering if Aarav could grow with the kids under your ashram."

"Good sir, I understand your apprehensions towards the boy's academics, but the step you are taking is very radical and needs some serious retrospection. You may find highly regarded intellectuals as your family's frontrunners on the professional front, but you are not going to find a soft spoken, kind-hearted pious man like Aarav anywhere else! Besides, why do you want to commit the sin of making your lovely son an orphan? Please reconsider your decision, and I am saying this not as the founder of the ashram, but as a well-wisher and your family friend. "

"People say some things are not in our hands, but that is not true. The real hard-spoken fact is that nothing is in our hands. It is all the play of the divine. We are just mere puppets."

"Are you disowning me?"

"Not if you pass the examinations."

"I cannot. Every subject feels like a mountain to climb. You have to understand me and my interests, I implore you."

"I don't want to hear any more nonsense from you, I have had enough of these cowardly excuses in your defence. Aren't you ashamed of yourself? Have you even tried studying wholeheartedly, at least for our family's honour?"

"I am ready to go to the ashram, if this is how it is going to be. I think I have committed way too many sins in my previous incarnation, which is why karma has struck me in this lifetime.

Meanwhile, I just find it astonishing that I have endured all of this for 18 long years.... Isn't that the greatest achievement in itself?"

Saying so, Aarav fell asleep abruptly in the living hall itself, his 6-feet body extending way beyond the sofa. The condition he was suffering from was narcolepsy, a rare sleeping disorder where strong emotions (such as sadness, laughter, or anger) can trigger sudden muscle weakness or even sleep episodes.

Kuldeep was taken aback and was in complete disarray of the words thrown at him by his son. He was speechless and was immersed in a state of frustration and melancholy as past memories from his own life flashed before his startled eyes...................................

I vividly still remember that instance where I understood that the world I lived in was something serene, joyous and completely blissful.

The key takeaway is that I am living one heck of a life. Not only me, each and every person on this land.

Although, making a statement that life here is easy is a misconception in itself. It may be true that there are equal opportunities here and everybody is treated the same irrespective of their economic/social status, but you still have to earn your bread, things don't come to you served on a golden platter.

However, people strive for excellence and enjoying working simply for the fact that work is directly proportional to efforts, which in turn is directly proportional to the rewards you reap. As simple as that. You work less, you get less, but you work more, you get more. No other way of interpreting it.

People are very happy here. So much so that people keep smiling and laughing all the time, be it them performing their daily chores, or even having a tough time at work! Be it success or be it failure, people embrace it with the same mindset. Of course, another thing to be noted here is that every person earns a living, and is content with his/her work. No one is greedy or no one is unhappy about things happening in their lives.

I still remember that I was, you know, not really a bright student right from my childhood days, and a testimony to that is my shabby speech and pronunciation until the age of 10! That's right, I could hardly talk properly until I was 10 years old, and what amuses me is the fact that I still stutter quite a few times while articulating some words, even though I am a well-grown 19-year-old lad. I have faced zero criticism for this and believe me or not, I was treated royally- because people around me felt that I was unique and being different was a good thing.

I really felt blessed to be part of such a group of compassionate people. This world was beautiful, God had curated it meticulously, to ensure no person remains in desolation, and everyone gets a fair share of their blissful and joyful moments. I would probably go to the extent of saying that perhaps God had been a bit more considerate towards me, as these 19 years- were nothing short of a dazzling and vibrant spectacle unfolded, with divine souls aka my parents making sure that I lived the life of a prince, while they put in the hard work.

VII

"Did you just say stressful? Do you even realise how easy it is and how you are making a fuss for no goddamn reason? You are one step away from joining a world-class institute for your engineering and this is what you have to say? How woeful. I should have not come to you now after I left you when you were 6 years old, if this is what I thought would happen"

Kuldeep swallowed gulps of water to make sure he developed more resilience, although he was having a collapsed state of mind and was broken from inside.

"Father, please try to understand my feelings, all that I am trying to say is that this is maybe not my cup of tea and I want to pursue something that..."

"Get one thing quite clear to your head young man, I am in charge of this house and the enormous weight of taking the family's reputation in excellence is bestowed upon my shoulders and you will have to carry this sooner or later. So, stop this rubbish chatter of yours and focus on things that actually matter, like securing a top rank in the examination that will propel you to one of the best institutes. Am I clear?"

"Y...yes father, I will try my level best and will not let you down."

"You cannot let me down son. Just remember the consequences-you will be termed incompetent and I will surely disown you, if that stage comes, as I cannot put the family's prestige at stake. Just remember that and you will never dream of failing in life. People say fear is bad, I say it is nonsense. Fear is very good, and now it is that fear of letting me down that will make you reach new heights in your endeavours."

"Of course, father, whatever you say."

This conversation summed up the state Kuldeep was in during his teenage, and this was what he encountered in his past. It was not something his son knew, and he wish he would tell him one day. Cut to present, the fear of failing to carry his family's legacy in Kuldeep's mind made sure he continued the act of dictatorship from his father, and it didn't look like this trend would die for generations to come.

Why, you ask? The FEAR of responsibility, the constant reminder about upholding the family's legacy. Perhaps it was okay to break the Mold, but the families were just, like, tuned in this system for hundreds of generations, and this was more like a tradition.

A tradition of excellence, some might say. A tradition of suffocating expectations, others might argue. Kuldeep was trapped in its endless loop, just as his father had been, and his grandfather before him. The weight of their collective achievements pressed down on him, a constant reminder of the impossibly high standards he had to maintain. It wasn't just about personal success anymore; it was about preserving the family's honour, their reputation, their very identity.

He remembered the countless hours he had spent studying, sacrificing his childhood, his dreams, his very essence for the sake of academic achievement. Sometimes he did not even realise why he was running behind excellence, like where was the journey heading? What was its real purpose? Just to keep up with the family's legacy? He decided not to think about such questions, as there was no space for rational thinking, where he could pause his life for a minute or two and contemplate the battle he was facing. There was no room for failure, no space for anything other than the relentless pursuit of excellence. The fear of disappointing his father, of being deemed unworthy, was a constant companion, a shadow that stretched long and dark behind him.

And now, he was passing that fear on to his own son. Aarav, who, with his gentle spirit and his artistic inclinations, was a stark contrast to the Sen legacy. But Kuldeep, blinded by tradition and fear, couldn't see that. He couldn't see the damage he was inflicting, the way he was crushing his son's spirit under the weight of his expectations.

He was so consumed by the fear of failure that he couldn't recognize the failure he was perpetrating. He was so obsessed with preserving the family's legacy that he was destroying the very thing he sought to protect: his son's happiness and peace of mind, the 2 things that should, IDEALLY, matter the most.........

It's about time that I start the journey by talking about my father, or should I say, "God-sent angel" or probably God himself.

Another thing to note is that my life story would not be narrated in a chronological order in which the events occurred, because I prefer saying the things that I first recall in my head. So, here goes one of the memorable events out of the whole lot.

This happened recently, after I successfully graduated from 10th grade, albeit not the grades worth boasting about. However, the grades didn't matter because all that people recognised was whether the student cleared all the subjects or not, and that I surely did.

Now, I had to take the next step, I had to plan out my future, what I would study, what are my interests, etc.

Here is where I found myself stuck in a web of options. There were just many things one could become that I lost track of what actually fascinated me. I couldn't make up my mind on what to do next, although one strong resolution was taken- I will not be trotting the conventional path of engineers, doctors, blah blah, because that was definitely not what my conscience wanted and that was certainly not my forte.

Nevertheless, I was really nervous to say this to my father. Don't take me wrong, it was not the fear of rejection, and it was not that my father was a dictator, if anything, he was exactly the opposite.

What was running in my mind, however, was the 'spark' I witnessed in him when he got to know that one of his friend's sons was pursuing engineering in a reputed institute. He had always listened to me and never said a word against my interests thus far. Thus, it would only be fair on my part that I do something to please him, and I would do anything in a heartbeat to make him happy. Anything.

Therefore, it was obvious that I was in two minds while deciding my career. The first plan was to give a break, get to know my actual interests and pursue them joyously. Another route would be to complete engineering in an institute for the heck of it, make my father happy and then decide what to do after engineering.

Though my mind inclined towards the second path, my heart pointed straight towards the first idea.

One thing that has always been a constant in the people of this world (at least the people I have witnessed so far) is that they always follow their heart, because no one is compelled by their parents and our society treats a shop-vendor, software engineer, or a writer the same way. It is the people who are valued here, not what they do.

Considering all these, I decided to tell my father that I would be taking a small break and go on a vacation. I wanted to explore.

"Dad, I wanted to say something."

"What is it, my dear son? Anything bugging you?"

"No, not at all. It's just that I decided that I would need some time for me to take my next step, and I do not want to pursue engineering or medicine for sure."

"That's my boy! Always thinking outside the box and bidding adieu to same old boring fields which have been there for decades together. I am really happy my son, and I am sure you will excel at whatever you do. What's more important for me, however, is that you always stay happy irrespective of the circumstances. If things are going too hard, just don't do it. Always remember that the ultimate goal in life is to enjoy every moment of it and be happy, because life doesn't come twice, at least that is what I believe in, so live life king size!

This was the conversation. That's all. Nothing more.

Sometimes I just keep wondering about how fortunate I am to ever have such a father and live such an amazing life. Well, to be honest, everybody living here is as fortunate as I am.

Once again, welcome to Amrit Nagar, a place that feels both surreal and strangely familiar, as if pulled from a forgotten dream............................

IX

Aarav got up, smiling. This was not unusual, as he started his day with a smile on his face, just after he woke up. The only period of time where Aarav felt really happy and joyous was for an hour or so just after waking up. After that, he slipped into depression and would not even move his facial muscles for the rest of the day.

He had faced numerous challenges owing to the sleeping disorder, due to obvious reasons.

Unfortunately, he had faced them in crucial junctures of his life. For instance, he had faced this disorder on the day of his final examinations of second semester, due to being extremely nervous and tensed before the exam. This resulted in him sleeping through the entire exam and even the constant efforts of the invigilator trying to wake him up paid no dividends.

Which is why he needs to now prepare for the supplementary exams set to commence shortly. For Aarav, this was torture, as he had slept for not one, but all examinations, and he had to take all of them now, again. He just hated the fact that he had to study again, and he thought to himself that he would trade places with anyone in this world, period.

Just then, he received a notification on his Gmail.

It was regarding a scriptwriting contest to be held in the college the next week. He opened the e-mail:

Greetings to all the students!!!

This is to inform all the enthusiastic and aspiring students about the scriptwriting contest being held next week. The top 3 scripts are going to win a cash price of 20,000 and also get an opportunity to meet the famous film director, Anuj!

Mode of submission: Online

So, what are you waiting for. Grab your opportunity to showcase your writing talent to the entire globe!

He was smiling the instant he finished reading the e-mail, however just seconds later, that smile disappeared and he slammed the phone on the desk with frustration.

Thud! A huge sound echoed the emotions of Aarav, filled with rage and fury.

This noise invited the wrath of his father.

Kuldeep (Alarmed): What was that sound?

Aarav did not speak a word.

Kuldeep: Are you studying for the exams? Or just passing time?

Again, there was no reply from Aarav.

Kuldeep: Why are you showing arrogance?

Aarav: I want to become a scriptwriter.

Kuldeep: What in the world?! Scriptwriter?

Aarav: I am passionate about it, it is something I really enjoy doing, here take a look at my writings if you want to, this is my personal diary and...

Kuldeep: Stop right there. This is just an excuse for you to quit academics, which again proves your incompetence and give-up attitude. Look, I want you passing the goddamn examinations and continue with your engineering, you get that?

Aarav gave a death stare at his father. And then just gave no reply as he thought it was for the better of both his and his father's mental peace.

X

So, what happened next is that my father purchased me a vehicle, and I couldn't be happier. I fell head over heels for it immediately—it was my first taste of true freedom. It was a beautiful machine, no doubt about that, in fact, I find all machines beautiful in their own way. Each has its own character to delve into, and every journey is an everlasting experience; an unforgettable moment of joy.

Now, speaking about my vehicle, I, for one, couldn't actually operate it well enough for the first few attempts. Repeated stumbles, awkward starts and stops, a general feeling of ineptitude. This was what made me question my thought of having it at the first place, and all the excitement and enthusiasm I had shown at the time of purchase slowly started to turn into gloom and worry.

My father could immediately notice that something was bothering me as soon as he observed my behaviour and mood during these first few days.

He came to me, gently stroking my head and asked me- "Are you having apprehensions about this now, my dear?"

I was genuinely surprised. How did my father make out what exactly was lingering in my mind?

"I am your father, son. I always know what you are thinking, always."

He heard this too!

"Father, I am just sad that I am not able to do it. I kind of regret this decision. Maybe I was not ready and just rushed the purchase."

"Ha Ha! Son, I don't know why, but I see myself in you. Even I had the exact same feeling when I first had something like this. I questioned myself- Am I even a fit for this? Did I make a mistake? However, fast forward a while later, I was an expert, heck I even went for long journeys and even was an active member of groups that were about it. So, one thing I realized at that point is that everything is going to be alright if you give some time to it. Be patient, and let things happen in their own pace.

Always remember, whenever you are stuck or feel lost in life-give some time and keep doing what you are supposed to do. Follow the process and have patience, that's all! And once you overcome the obstacle that is bothering you, trust me, the feeling is surreal-it is what life is all about."

I would never forget these words of my father, and keep reminiscing it every time I feel low or lost.

I think you would have understood by now what happened next. I got a good grip on my new found freedom, and like my father, could go to long trips and was having the time of my life. Nothing like having this, it is a companion for life. It was a symbol of more than just transport, it was a symbol of more mature relationship with my father.

Just after this trip, however, a life-changing moment had just occurred for me.... A moment that would make me question everything I thought I knew about my world and the people in it.

XI

Aarav just couldn't take it anymore. To escape the torment of his father, he found no option but to run away. However, what if his father accepted him if he passed the examinations? Then he would have no problem, maybe he could pursue his passion after engineering with the approval of his father.

After a solid 5-6 minutes of being in two minds about this, he finally decided to sneak away as he was quite sure that his father would never change his ways, and that his incompetence in studies was just a medium for his father to demean him. According to Aarav, things would have been the same, even if he would have been the state's topper, as his father was never satisfied and always craving for more success and fame.

Just then, he realised, he couldn't survive outside either. He was not financially independent, on top of that, he was an introvert and there was no way he could imagine himself living on the streets, given that he was from an affluent family.

Days passed by, the supplementary exams came up, and as unfortunate as it can get, Aarav failed in these too, albeit he was awake this time and tried his best. Engineering was probably not his cup of tea, he thought. Also, he was not the least surprised about the result, as he for one, knew that there was nothing more complicated and terrifying for him to understand than academics.

A sense of disgust started to appear on Aarav's face and the pathetic condition he was in.

"HOW ARE YOU SO INCOMPETENT!? CAN'T YOU DO ONE THING, RIGHT?"

He shouted at the top of his lungs. He found no reason to live. No respect from his father, let alone the society, also now he was really proving to be a liability to his father, at least, that's what his father always thought about him.

He then heard footsteps, and they only became louder and louder.

It was his father. He banged on the door with a large thud, Aarav could feel his rage even when the door was closed.

"Aarav, you imbecile! Open the goddamn door!"

Aarav was so scared to handle the gravitas of the situation that he started developing heart palpitations, and suddenly collapsed to the floor.

"I said, open the goddamn door, you idiot!"

Observing no reply of any sorts, Aarav's father breaks open the door with huge force, only to witness something very unexpected.......

XII

A lecture being delivered on the topic "Universal Human Values"

"What makes us truly human? Is it intelligence? Creativity? Or is it the values that shape our thoughts, decisions, and actions?

Throughout history, societies have flourished or collapsed based on the values they upheld. Justice, compassion, honesty, respect—these are not just words but guiding principles that define how we interact with others, make ethical decisions, and build a harmonious world. In today's lecture, we explore these principles, not as abstract ideals, but as practical foundations for a fulfilling life."

Aarav didn't have any friends at all, as no person in his class felt academics was something so difficult except Aarav. The general consensus was that Aarav was just a dimwit, and deserved no place in the institution. His performance was only pulling the legacy of the institute backward, at least, that's what the so called 'peer group' of the presumed 'top' college thought.

However, no one cared to listen to the ongoing lecture, even the toppers, as they felt there were much better things they could do. Many people didn't attend the lectures of this particular course, they either went to library or some of them just sleepwalked through the class just for the sole intention of fulfilling the 'attendance criteria'.

The amusing part of this was that Aarav enjoyed these lectures a lot, and seemed to really connect to the course. Every word the professor said seemed to him as if the course was made for him.

He also shone in all the activities related to this particular subject-be it quizzes, tests, anything related to the subject. The only subject which he could closely relate to, and feel at home with.

Therefore, it was of no surprise that he developed a good rapport with the professor, exchanging stories, sharing moments of anger, frustration and so on that took place in his horrid phase of life.

The professor too, was very open-minded, practical, and compassionate. He was all ears for Aarav's complaints and perspective towards life. He started to adore Aarav's calm demeanour and nature.

The professor was deeply moved by Aarav's plight at home. The fact that he had to undergo such a rigorous phase at such a young age, didn't sit well with the professor.

The professor decided that something had to be done, he couldn't let a person of Aarav's quality, forget the man he actually could be. He just had a different purpose, a different cause to fulfil, and clearly engineering was not what was written in his destiny. He spent many sleepless nights thinking about Aarav and the situations he had to encounter, and finally one day it seemed like he found a one-of-a-kind solution to bring life back to Aarav's listless world.

One thing was for certain-the professor vowed to change Aarav's life-for the better, however no one knew what plan was cooked up under the sleeve.

What was the professor up to?

XIII

"Would you like to have a break, sir? You seem to be stressed out and nervous", said the lady.

The funny thing is, I don't know where I am, what I am doing and who on earth is this lady.

The biggest doubt on the top my mind, why would anybody call me sir? I have not accomplished any milestone in life yet, apart from being a sore loser in front of my father.

Also, why does place look leaps and bounds beautiful than the actual place, I am supposed to be in?

What is this place?

"Sir? Are you alright? You seem anxious."

"I...err...uh...mmm..."

"Do you need a glass of water? Seems like the enormous success of the books you have written has overwhelmed you with happiness sir, you are almost a celebrity now."

This lady is being very polite to me, which is refreshing. I quite like the way I am getting treated.

Now, another nightmarish thought is creeping into my head. Am I in an orphanage? Nah, there is no way an orphanage would look this vibrant and elegant in my part of the city. This place straight up looks like an adaptation of

Disneyland. Is this the other part of the city?

I was probably kidnapped, human trafficking maybe?

Alright, now there is only one way to know where I am. I need to ask this lady, but wait, she isn't even letting me speak-

"I can drive you to your favourite view spot of you would like sir, you seem a bit anxious. Or maybe listen to all the praises people have to say about your books. Maybe you just want a stroll in the garden? Or sir, maybe you just need some rest. You have been working quite rigorously for your age, creating such a huge sensation at such an age is not an easy task at all."

WHERE WAS I? WHAT IS THIS PLACE?

"Do you want to have your favourite soup? I can get it done in a few minutes. Perhaps you want freshly pressed juice. That too shall be served. Whatever makes you feel comfortable."

I would be comfortable if you let me speak, kind lady! I really need to know what is going on.

"Oh, and congrats for a million sales, sir! I just heard about it in the morning. You truly are one gem of a writer, I must say. There is some hidden magic wand in those hands when you start writing, leading to the spell-bounding stories you write. Just unbelievably good!"

CAN YOU STOP TALKING FOR A MINUTE!

"Uhh...actually I need to know"

"Where your father is? He will be here any moment now, I think all that he needs is 5 more minutes before the call ends, after which, I myself will call him here."

Wait a minute. Where exactly am I? What happened to me?

This place doesn't seem like...home.

Why is the place so awkwardly silent? Is this place haunted? What is going on?

"Wake up!"

That's my father's voice. Thank God he is here. What's it with the shouting though? Why have we moved to this place? Maybe a new investment on a house, perhaps? My father probably wanted to surprise me with a new house. Yes, that is all must have happened. What else can happen in this beautiful, harmless world?

"Wow, what a surprise, father! The last time I checked we were in a different house! Although I must agree that I love the surprise and this house appears much more pleasing to the eye."

"What do you mean? Playing games with me?"

I was appalled to hear my father's tone. Why was my father talking like this? Something didn't seem right.

The sensible thing to do would be to go to the living room and affirm, whether this was really my father.

"Father? Is that you?"

"Yes."

Okay, now this is indeed him. Why is he speaking in such a tone?

"Is everything okay, father?"

"You tell me, you dimwit. Do you realise how much you are tarnishing the golden reputation our family enjoys in the field of education? Each of our ancestors have excelled in various fields, including Vedas, mathematics, science and so on. People have looked up to their teachings and they were the torchbearers of their generation in their respective fields. They were driven by a passion to succeed and outgrow perfection in their line of work. This humongous responsibility of carrying such a prestigious legacy forward was bestowed upon my shoulders by my father, and I can confidently say that, I have put all the steps in the right direction.

Now, it is the future generation that scares me. I mean, look at you, zero responsibility towards achieving a respectable degree. Tell me, what is that you actually have in store to prove your mettle? To top all of this, none of the professors or fellow mates have a good opinion on you, all of them think you are just a worthless junk. The icing on the cake is that one stupid writing habit of yours, where you write all useless things no one cares about.

All this actually makes me ponder if you are actually my son. I definitely did not want my son to turn out like this."

I just couldn't believe my father said that. I was totally devastated. I was in loss of words. I know my father had a huge legacy, but I was of the opinion that he wanted me to pursue whatever I yearned and loved doing. I did not know all this was hidden deep inside him. So, all the love he showered me with all these years was all a lie! He was just waiting for the right moment to burst at me.

Here I was thinking that he was an angel sent to keep me happy forever, but this outburst was so painful to bear. The fact that my father agreed to follow my dreams at that point and is now talking in contrast to that day just baffles me. Also, the fact that I am now successful in my path, being the youngest millionaire in the country, and my father, disregarding all this, wanted to just fire at me all of a sudden!

"B...but F...father...you...gave..."

"What is it with that stuttering! Speak properly!"

I couldn't take this anymore. I started weeping, and trust me, I never knew what weeping looked like, before this moment. All the beautiful moments spent these 19 years felt like a myth.

Not able to handle the heat of the situation, I collapsed onto the floor. After spending my life in deemed-to-be heaven for 19 years, this was undeniably my entry into hell, an entry I never asked for, in life.

The second before I fainted, and when my mind was still active before fizzling out, I just had one thought popping up in my head-

WHOEVER CREATED THE GODDAMN MESS, BETTER STRAIGHTEN THINGS UP!

IF NOT, THIS HAD BETTER JUST BE A BAD DREAM!

A case that was related to the kidnap of the Police officer's own son was grabbing headlines in the city. He was found missing for 2 days now, and the Police officer decided to question every person associated with his son. By doing so, he found a major suspect.

The suspect was the universal human values professor of an engineering college, which was in no way, related to his son. However, this man was not only a professor, but also a scientist.

In the interrogation chamber:

Policeman: So, tell me, why did you do this?

Scientist: It wouldn't have happened this way, had the wretch pressed the goddamn button on time.

Policeman: The what exactly?

Scientist: A red button whose significance lingers in the air, unspoken yet undeniably crucial., exactly halfway through the film. Oh no, I guess I have spoken a bit too much. Blame the tongue.

Policeman: Film? I thought you were a a scientist whose eyes seem to hold secrets far beyond the realm of ordinary comprehension.

Scientist: I am actually a professor who teaches universal human values too to engineering students if that gives me some brownie points.

Policeman: Universal Human Values? A scientist whose eyes seem to hold secrets far beyond the realm of ordinary comprehension.? You ought to be kidding me. On one hand, you conduct hazardous experiments with utter disdain for the people of this country, and on the other, you preach about ethics! You two-faced crook!

Scientist: Hey, calm your nerves, officer! I am not that kind of a a scientist, I am a film scientist.

Policeman: Huh? Now what in the world is a film a scientist? Sounds like a weird fusion of fields.

Scientist: It's complicated, can't exactly brief out what I do.

Policeman: You better try to, pal, if you want a way out of this.

Scientist: Now that I think about it, it's not even that complicated. I am a a scientist predominantly conducting experiments on the films I craft and direct.

Policeman: What kind of experiments are those?

Scientist: That stays with me till the rest of my life, no offence.

Policeman: Offence taken. You need to tell me everything!

Scientist: Nope, I am not telling you, I am sorry. Just ask me anything else but that.

Policeman: Where is my son?!

Scientist: I can't answer that too. It's...complicated.

Policeman: Trust me, you don't want be in prison all your life. And you don't want to hide things from me, especially about my own son.

Scientist: That's true, officer. But believe me, there is no way you are going to fall for what I say now. It is too surreal to be true. As much as you value your son's life, you must value my story too, only then can we bring your son back, and maybe, things will get back to normal.

Policeman: I have heard enough tales to believe what you say, trust me. You just have to let it out, and mind you, you do not have a choice. So, tell me, who are you? What do you actually do? What did you do to my son? I want every goddamn detail.

Scientist: Sigh... okay then, here goes my story.......

XVI

"And the best actor award for this year goes to...Vikram!"

Huge standing ovation from the crowd, as Vikram comes towards the stage to collect his award, waving his hands in admiration to the crowd.

"I am beyond ecstatic to be holding the award for my first ever film as a lead actor. I sincerely thank my parents, for supporting me in every ounce and making me the man I am today...."

Just then-

"Vikram, wake up, it's already 7 AM! Oh god, see the plight of today's generation! Imagine aspiring to be an IAS officer and still snoring on the bed!"

Vikram grunted, rolling over to face the wall. "Just five more minutes, Pa," he mumbled, his voice thick with sleep.

"Five more minutes, huh?" His father scoffed. "That's what you say every morning. And then you end up being late for coaching, or worse, missing it altogether."

Vikram knew his father was right, but the allure of sleep was too strong to resist. He closed his eyes, drifting back to his dream.

"Vikram!" His father's voice was sharp, laced with impatience. "Get up this instant, or I swear..."

Vikram groaned, finally dragging himself out of bed. He glanced at the clock - 7:15 AM. He was going to be late again.

As he rushed to get ready, his mind wandered back to his dream. He had always wanted to be an actor, but his father had other plans for him. He wanted Vikram to follow in his footsteps, to become a respected officer of the law.

Vikram sighed. He knew he couldn't disappoint his father, but the thought of spending his life behind a desk, pushing papers and interrogating criminals, made him cringe. He longed for the stage, for the chance to bring characters to life and transport audiences to different worlds.

He tried to broach the subject with his father once, but the conversation didn't go well. His father had brushed off his dreams, telling him to focus on his studies and secure a stable future.

"There's no future in acting," his father had said. "It's a fickle industry, full of uncertainty and rejection. You need a real job, something that will provide for you and your family."

Vikram had tried to argue, to explain his passion, but his father wouldn't listen. He was adamant that Vikram should follow his chosen path, and that was the end of it.

From that day on, Vikram kept his dreams to himself, burying them deep inside his heart. He went through the motions of studying, attending classes, and preparing for the IAS exams, but his heart wasn't in it.

One day, after a particularly gruelling session of exam preparation, Vikram decided he'd had enough. He couldn't take it anymore. He needed to escape, to find a place where he could be himself, where he could pursue his dreams without fear of judgment or disapproval.

He packed a bag, leaving a note for his parents, apologizing for disappointing them but explaining that he needed to follow his own path. Then, he slipped out of the house, disappearing into the maze of Mumbai's streets.

He wandered aimlessly for hours, lost and alone, but also strangely liberated. As night fell, he found himself in a deserted part of the city, where old warehouses and abandoned buildings lined the streets. He stumbled upon a strange-looking studio, with a brightly lit sign that read "Dreams Unlimited."

Curiosity piqued, he pushed open the door and stepped inside. The studio was a chaotic mix of props, costumes, and film equipment. In the centre of the room, a man with a kind face and gentle eyes was tinkering with a strange contraption.

"Welcome to Dreams Unlimited," the man said, a warm smile gracing his lips. "I'm a film scientist, and I can help make your dreams a reality."

Vikram was intrigued. "You can make my dreams come true?" he asked. "How?"

"I create films that come to life," the scientist explained. "They're not just movies; they're experiences. I understand you have a passion for acting, which is why you have entered this studio but your circumstances make it difficult to pursue. I can offer you a unique opportunity."

Vikram's heart raced. Could this be the answer to his prayers? A chance to finally act, to escape the life his father had planned for him?

"What kind of opportunity?" he asked eagerly.

"I have a film world," the scientist said, gesturing towards the contraption. "A place where you can live your dream, experience it fully. There is a certain plot I have crafted and you will be the protagonist of the film, however here you are literally living the role, i.e., the character you are playing is what you truly are, and you will have no association with the real world then, with a twist- You'll enter the film world for a set period – exactly half the film's runtime – and then you'll return to your normal life."

Vikram was hesitant. "Half the film? What happens then?"

The scientist avoided direct eye contact. "There's a process," he said vaguely. "A way to bring you back. The important thing is, you get to live your dream. You get to *act*. Isn't that what you want?"

Vikram thought of his father's disapproval, the stifling expectations, the feeling of his dreams slipping away. The scientist was right. This was his chance.

"Okay," he said, making his decision. "I'll do it."

The scientist beamed. "Excellent! You won't regret this. Just step into the machine. It will take you to the film world. "

"You say I get teleported to the film world, then how is that doing me any good and getting me recognition? Will this film be released in this world? Will I come back to this world and get the fame I deserve? Also, is it safe to do so? I might be an idiot to actually believe such things, but all this is coming from the passion I have towards acting."

"Yes, of course this is possible, you will become an overnight star! Don't worry," he added, a touch too quickly, "it's perfectly safe. Just sit back and enjoy the ride."

Little did Vikram know that the scientist, while kind-hearted, hadn't been entirely forthcoming. He hadn't mentioned the specific "clauses" of the return process, the intricacies of the switch, or the potential consequences if things went awry. He genuinely wanted to help Vikram achieve his dream, but he also needed someone passionate, someone willing to take the leap. And he knew Vikram's desire to act was so strong, he wouldn't ask too many questions.

XVII

Scientist: I am a film scientist as I already said before. Now I am not going to delve into the philanthropic activities I might have done through my noble profession, as we do not have much time and that is definitely not the need of the hour.

Policeman: Right.

Scientist: Okay, moving on, so basically, I made an invention involving some sophisticated concepts of physics like the "Resonance Point" theory.

Policeman: Oh, the things I have to endure for my son, never dreamt of having a physics lecture in an interrogation chamber. Regardless, please continue.

Scientist: I would be grateful if you wouldn't intervene in my explanation.

Policeman: Whatever.

Scientist (sulks a bit): Anyways, where was I? Ah... the "Resonance Point" theory. As I discussed earlier, I crafted films that came to life, but how would I achieve swapping of souls, i.e. the soul exchange? This is where I used this concept.

Imagine that every person's consciousness has a unique "vibration" or "frequency," like a musical note. This is their "resonance."

After relentless pursuit, the advanced film technology I have designed can capture and store this resonance, not just the visual and auditory aspects of a person. It's like recording the very essence of their being and existence.

This resonance is what makes the film world more than just a movie; it's a living, breathing reality.

So, when I create my film, I am essentially building a "resonance matrix." This matrix holds the resonances of all the characters and the environment.

The film world isn't static. It evolves and changes based on the interactions of these resonances.

The matrix can be altered and manipulated with, by adding or removing resonances, and even altering their frequencies.

Within the film's narrative, there's a specific moment where the resonance matrix reaches a peak of stability and coherence. This is the "resonance point." Think of it as the moment when all the elements of the film world are perfectly aligned, creating a harmonious and powerful resonance.

After multiple trials and days of experimentation, I found out that this lies exactly halfway through the film, where the film's reality reaches a peak of stability. You can draw parallels to that of a sound wave concept, as of how a sound wave reaches its peak amplitude at a certain point.

This resonance point is pre-programmed into the film's structure, like a hidden trigger. The activation "trigger" here is the red button I was talking about.

The "button" sends out a signal that matches the peak frequency, triggering the swap, when pressed at the right interval, i.e., exactly halfway through.

However, when the button is pressed at the wrong time, it causes an interference pattern, like when two sound waves are out of sync, and that this interference is what causes the swap to fail.

Look, now I am quite sure this sounds like Greek and Latin to you, but it is what it is.

Unfortunately, the button was pressed at the wrong time, leading to the mishap.

Policeman: I want to know why my son did what he did, with a madman like you! There was no need for him to do that! I just wish he is safe. If something happens to him, I ...

Scientist: Trust me, tough man. He is going to be fine, just listen to me....

"Just you wait sir, let me call your father."

"Did you just say you would call my father? No no, wait!"

Too late! The supposedly kind lady went away to bring my father, which was the last thing I would want now.

What is he going to do now? I have failed my supplementary examinations as well. Is he going to throw me out of the house? Is he going to disown me and throw me in an orphanage. Oh, I cannot even imagine myself in these circumstances. Oh, how desolate is my state now!

Just then, both the lady and my father came marching towards me. I was scared out of my wits to see my father.

"F...fa...ther, I am terribly sorry, I do not mean to be a liability to ..."

I saw my father smile! Never in my life did I see him don such a cheerful face, full of warmth. Seeing his face like this reminded me of a god sent angel.

"What are you talking about, my dear son? You are the greatest price I have ever possessed in my entire lifetime thus far! I love you so much, and it just pains me to see you think that way. I am really sorry if any of my actions made you feel that way. Here, have this juice."

I took the glass and was dumbfounded. Does my father have two faces? Why was he being so polite. The sudden showering of love and affection made me feel a bit uncomfortable. It felt too good to be true. Well, I think I should stop dreaming. Let me pinch myself. There! I hope I am back to my normal life now.

Okay, my father is still cheerful and the lady is also still present. So, is this really not a dream after all? Has God answered my prayers or is my father planning something under the sleeve?

"I love you, my son. Come on, let us go on a ride together on your bike. That should ease you out."

I have a bike??????!!!!!

I really hope this is not a dream; all this just feels too good to be true. If things have really changed for the better, I, uh, can't thank God enough for this.

I thought of cherishing these moments to the maximum, as no one knew what would happen henceforth, with the wildly dwindling nature of my father.

"Of course, father, I would be privileged to have a bike ride with you."

"You seem to become humble day by day, my son. You seem to forget the millionaire you have become already, which is a rare sight these days. Always stay grounded this way."

These were enough twists to encounter in a lifetime. Did my father just say that I became a millionaire? How? Did he just pass on his assets in my name? I couldn't just comprehend this scenario.

"Forgive me, but I don't understand how I have become a milliona.."

"Now there sir, he is becoming too humble, don't you think? He even forgot the fact that he has become a millionaire, thanks to which I was able to find a job as a caretaker in this beautiful

house and sustain my family. I cannot thank both of you enough, as I feel this is my responsibility rather than a chore, and never have I felt like a stranger in this house.

Okay now, at least I have an answer to who the kind lady was, but the funny thing is, I don't understand how things took such a big turn without me remembering the massive flow of events that have taken place in the span of, what, like 24 hours, I guess? Perhaps even shorter.

The scenario screams fantasy, as if me and my father were pushed into a different backdrop, and my father was turned into a new leaf by whoever so thought it was a great idea to do so. Maybe it is just that I deserved all this? Maybe there is lot of light after a overhauling spell of darkness? Or if I were being absolutely pessimistic, maybe this is just hallucination and my father is screaming at the top of his lungs?

Just when I was lost in my stream of never-ending thoughts, I was in the parking lot, witnessing my so-called bike, without me knowing what bike it was. All that I can say is that it looked good and nothing much. I really liked the colour, but that's about it. I never really had put my mind into motorcycles so can't really explain anything else.

"Come on son, hop on and let's go!"

Huh? Am I supposed to be the one riding it? I am not sure how this machine works. Are these the brake levers? Why are there switches on the handlebar? First of all, how do I start this motorcycle?

"What's the matter son, anything wrong with the bike?"

How was I supposed to say that the problem was not the bike, but me! I wouldn't want to let down my father, who trusts me and wants me to ride the bike. On the other hand, I don't think I know even the fundamentals of how a bike works and how to get this thing moving. Not knowing what to do, I just fainted out of nervousness. Well not exactly nervousness I suppose, it was a mixture of extreme ecstasy, joy and the nervousness all weaved together in high doses. If not for that narcolepsy, I would have been riding my bike all over the streets with my father.

However, before I doze off, I say this again- I HOPE THIS IS NOT A DREAM!!

TO BE CONTINUED

EPILOGUE

Two lives. Two different realities. Two unexpected paths. No one knew what was in store.

On one hand, there was AmritNagar—a world that breathed positivity, embracing all who entered.

On the other, the same old world—filled with struggles, uncertainty, and the weight of impossible expectations.

Who was in AmritNagar? What exactly was this place? These questions haunted two souls, trapped between fate and choice.

But one thing was certain—this was just the beginning. Something unprecedented. Something extraordinary.

www.ingramcontent.com/pod-product-compliance
Lightning Source LLC
LaVergne TN
LVHW040955150826
845672LV00002B/720

9798897448388